Edward C Caswell

OLD NEW YORK

FALSE DAWN

(The 'Forties)

By EDITH WHARTON

OLD NEW YORK
   FALSE DAWN
   THE OLD MAID
   THE SPARK
   NEW YEAR'S DAY

THE GLIMPSES OF THE MOON

THE AGE OF INNOCENCE

SUMMER

THE REEF

THE MARNE

FRENCH WAYS AND THEIR MEANING

OLD NEW YORK

FALSE DAWN

(*The 'Forties*)

BY

EDITH WHARTON

AUTHOR OF "THE AGE OF INNOCENCE," ETC.

DECORATIONS BY E. C. CASWELL

D. APPLETON AND COMPANY
NEW YORK :: LONDON :: MCMXXIV

FALSE DAWN

(The 'Forties)

PART I

FALSE DAWN

(The 'Forties)

I

HAY, verbena and mignonette scented the languid July day. Large strawberries, crimsoning through sprigs of mint, floated in a bowl of pale yellow cup on the verandah table: an old Georgian bowl, with complex reflections on polygonal flanks, engraved with the Ray‹cie arms between lions' heads. Now and again the gentlemen, warned by a menacing hum, slapped their cheeks, their brows or their bald crowns; but they did so as furtively as possible, for Mr. Halston Raycie, on whose verandah they sat, would not admit that there were mosquitoes at High Point.

The strawberries came from Mr. Raycie's kitchen garden; the Georgian bowl came from his great-grandfather (father of the Signer); the verandah was that of his country-house, which stood on a height above the Sound, at a convenient driving distance from his town house in Canal Street.

"Another glass, Commodore," said Mr. Raycie, shaking out a cambric handkerchief the size of a table-cloth, and applying a corner of it to his steaming brow. Mr. Jameson Ledgely smiled and took another glass. He was known as "the Commodore" among his intimates because of having been in the Navy in his youth, and having taken part, as a midshipman under Admiral Porter, in the war of 1812. This jolly sunburnt bachelor, whose face

resembled that of one of the bronze idols
he might have brought back with him, had
kept his naval air, though long retired
from the service; and his white duck
trousers, his gold-braided cap and shining
teeth, still made him look as if he might
be in command of a frigate. Instead of
that, he had just sailed over a party of
friends from his own place on the Long
Island shore; and his trim white sloop was
now lying in the bay below the point.

The Halston Raycie house overlooked
a lawn sloping to the Sound. The lawn
was Mr. Raycie's pride: it was mown
with a scythe once a fortnight, and rolled
in the spring by an old white horse spe-
cially shod for the purpose. Below the
verandah the turf was broken by three
round beds of rose-geranium, heliotrope
and Bengal roses, which Mrs. Raycie
tended in gauntlet gloves, under a small

hinged sunshade that folded back on its
carved ivory handle. The house, re-
modelled and enlarged by Mr. Raycie on
his marriage, had played a part in the
Revolutionary war as the settler's cottage
where Benedict Arnold had had his
headquarters. A contemporary print
of it hung in Mr. Raycie's study; but no
one could have detected the humble out-
line of the old house in the majestic stone-
coloured dwelling built of tongued-and-
grooved boards, with an angle tower, tall
narrow windows, and a verandah on cham-
fered posts, that figured so confidently as
a "Tuscan Villa" in Downing's "Landscape Gardening in America." There
was the same difference between the rude
lithograph of the earlier house and the fine
steel engraving of its successor (with a
"specimen" weeping beech on the lawn)
as between the buildings themselves. Mr.

[6]

Raycie had reason to think well of his architect.

He thought well of most things related to himself by ties of blood or interest. No one had ever been quite sure that he made Mrs. Raycie happy, but he was known to have the highest opinion of her. So it was with his daughters, Sarah Anne and Mary Adeline, fresher replicas of the lymphatic Mrs. Raycie; no one would have sworn that they were quite at ease with their genial parent, yet every one knew how loud he was in their praises. But the most remarkable object within the range of Mr. Raycie's self-approval was his son Lewis. And yet, as Jameson Ledgely, who was given to speaking his mind, had once observed, you wouldn't have supposed young Lewis was exactly the kind of craft Halston would have

turned out if he'd had the designing of
his son and heir.

Mr. Raycie was a monumental man.
His extent in height, width and thickness
was so nearly the same that whichever
way he was turned one had an almost
equally broad view of him; and every inch
of that mighty circumference was so ex-
quisitely cared for that to a farmer's eye
he might have suggested a great agricul-
tural estate of which not an acre is un-
tilled. Even his baldness, which was in
proportion to the rest, looked as if it
received a special daily polish; and on a
hot day his whole person was like some
wonderful example of the costliest irri-
gation. There was so much of him, and
he had so many planes, that it was fas-
cinating to watch each runnel of moisture follow its own particular watershed.
Even on his large fresh-looking hands the

drops divided, trickling in different ways from the ridges of the fingers; and as for his forehead and temples, and the raised cushion of cheek beneath each of his lower lids, every one of these slopes had its own particular stream, its hollow pools and sudden cataracts; and the sight was never unpleasant, because his whole vast bubbling surface was of such a clean and hearty pink, and the exuding moisture so perceptibly flavoured with expensive eau de Cologne and the best French soap.

Mrs. Raycie, though built on a less heroic scale, had a pale amplitude which, when she put on her best watered silk (the kind that stood alone), and framed her countenance in the innumerable blonde lace ruffles and clustered purple grapes of her newest Paris cap, almost balanced her husband's bulk. Yet from this full-rigged pair, as the Commodore would have put it, had issued the lean little runt of a Lewis, a shrimp of a baby, a shaver of a boy, and now a youth as scant as an ordinary man's midday shadow.

All these things, Lewis himself mused, dangling his legs from the verandah rail, were undoubtedly passing through the minds of the four gentlemen grouped about his father's bowl of cup.

Mr. Robert Huzzard, the banker, a tall broad man, who looked big in any company but Mr. Raycie's, leaned back, lifted his glass, and bowed to Lewis.

"Here's to the Grand Tour!"

"Don't perch on that rail like a sparrow, my boy," Mr. Raycie said reprovingly; and Lewis dropped to his feet, and returned Mr. Huzzard's bow.

"I wasn't thinking," he stammered. It was his too frequent excuse.

Mr. Ambrose Huzzard, the banker's younger brother, Mr. Ledgely and Mr. Donaldson Kent, all raised their glasses and cheerily echoed: "The Grand Tour!"

Lewis bowed again, and put his lips to the glass he had forgotten. In reality, he had eyes only for Mr. Donaldson Kent, his father's cousin, a silent man with a lean hawk-like profile, who looked like a retired Revolutionary hero, and lived in daily fear of the most trifling risk or responsibility.

To this prudent and circumspect citizen had come, some years earlier, the unexpected and altogether inexcusable demand that he should look after the daughter of his only brother, Julius Kent. Julius had died in Italy—well, that was his own business, if he chose to live there. But to let his wife die before him, and to leave a minor daughter, and a will entrusting her to the guardianship of his esteemed elder brother, Donaldson Kent Esquire, of Kent's Point, Long Island, and Great Jones Street, New York—well, as Mr. Kent himself said, and as his wife said for him, there had never been anything, anything whatever, in Mr. Kent's attitude or behaviour, to justify the ungrateful Julius (whose debts he had more than once paid) in laying on him this final burden.

The girl came. She was fourteen, she was considered plain, she was small and black and skinny. Her name was Beatrice, which was bad enough, and made worse by the fact that it had been shortened by ignorant foreigners to Treeshy. But she was eager, serviceable and good-tempered, and as Mr. and Mrs. Kent's friends pointed out, her plainness made everything easy. There were two Kent boys growing up, Bill and Donald; and

if this penniless cousin had been com-
pounded of cream and roses—well, she
would have taken more watching, and
might have rewarded the kindness of her
uncle and aunt by some act of wicked in-
gratitude. But this risk being obviated
by her appearance, they could be goodnatured to her without afterthought, and
to be goodnatured was natural to them.
So, as the years passed, she gradually became the guardian of her guardians; since
it was equally natural to Mr. and Mrs.
Kent to throw themselves in helpless reli-
ance on every one whom they did not
nervously fear or mistrust.

"Yes, he's off on Monday," Mr. Raycie
said, nodding sharply at Lewis, who had
set down his glass after one sip. "Empty
it, you shirk!" the nod commanded; and
Lewis, throwing back his head, gulped
down the draught, though it almost stuck

in his lean throat. He had already had
to take two glasses, and even this scant
conviviality was too much for him, and
likely to result in a mood of excited volubility, followed by a morose evening and
a head the next morning. And he wanted
to keep his mind clear that day, and to
think steadily and lucidly of Treeshy
Kent.

Of course he couldn't marry her—yet.
He was twenty-one that very day, and
still entirely dependent on his father.
And he wasn't altogether sorry to be
going first on this Grand Tour. It was
what he had always dreamed of, pined
for, from the moment when his infant eyes
had first been drawn to the prints of
European cities in the long upper passage
that smelt of matting. And all that
Treeshy had told him about Italy had
confirmed and intensified the longing.

[14]

Oh, to have been going there with her—
with her as his guide, his Beatrice! (For
she had given him a little Dante of her
father's, with a steel-engraved frontis-
piece of Beatrice; and his sister Mary
Adeline, who had been taught Italian by
one of the romantic Milanese exiles, had
helped her brother out with the gram-
mar.)

The thought of going to Italy with
Treeshy was only a dream; but later, as
man and wife, they would return there,
and by that time, perhaps, it was Lewis
who would be her guide, and reveal to her
the historic marvels of her birthplace, of
which after all she knew so little, except in
minor domestic ways that were quaint but
unimportant.

The prospect swelled her suitor's
bosom, and reconciled him to the idea of
their separation. After all, he secretly

felt himself to be still a boy, and it was as a man that he would return: he meant to tell her that when they met the next day. When he came back his character would be formed, his knowledge of life (which he already thought considerable) would be complete; and then no one could keep them apart. He smiled in advance to think how little his father's shouting and booming would impress a man on his return from the Grand Tour. . .

The gentlemen were telling anecdotes about their own early experiences in Europe. None of them—not even Mr. Raycie—had travelled as extensively as it was intended that Lewis should; but the two Huzzards had been twice to England on banking matters, and Commodore Ledgely, a bold man, to France and Belgium as well—not to speak of his early experiences in the Far East. All three

had kept a vivid and amused recollection, slightly tinged with disapproba-
tion, of what they had seen— "Oh, those
French wenches," the Commodore chuckled through his white teeth—but poor
Mr. Kent, who had gone abroad on his
honeymoon, had been caught in Paris by
the revolution of 1830, had had the fever
in Florence, and had nearly been arrested
as a spy in Vienna; and the only satisfactory episode in this disastrous, and never
repeated, adventure, had been the fact of
his having been mistaken for the Duke
of Wellington '(as he was trying to slip
out of a Viennese hotel in his courier's
blue surtout) by a crowd who had been—
"Well, very gratifying in their enthu-
siasm," Mr. Kent admitted.

"How my poor brother Julius could
have lived in Europe! Well, look at the
consequences—" he used to say, as if poor

Treeshy's plainness gave an awful point to his moral.

"There's one thing in Paris, my boy, that you must be warned against: those gambling-hells in the Pally Royle," Mr. Kent insisted. "I never set foot in the places myself; but a glance at the outside was enough."

"I knew a feller that was fleeced of a fortune there," Mr. Henry Huzzard confirmed; while the Commodore, at his tenth glass, chuckled with moist eyes: "The trollops, oh, the trollops—"

"As for Vienna—" said Mr. Kent.

"Even in London," said Mr. Ambrose Huzzard, "a young man must be on his look-out against gamblers. Every form of swindling is practised, and the touts are always on the look-out for greenhorns; a term," he added apologetically, "which they apply to any traveller new to the country."

"In Paris," said Mr. Kent, "I was once within an ace of being challenged to fight a duel." He fetched a sigh of horror and relief, and glanced reassuredly down the Sound in the direction of his own peaceful roof-tree.

"Oh, a duel," laughed the Commodore. "A man can fight duels here. I fought a dozen when I was a young feller in New Erleens." The Commodore's mother had been a southern lady, and after his father's death had spent some years with her parents in Louisiana, so that her son's varied experiences had begun early. " 'Bout women," he smiled confidentially, holding out his empty glass to Mr. Raycie.

"The ladies—!" exclaimed Mr. Kent in a voice of warning.

The gentlemen rose to their feet, the

Commodore quite as promptly and steadily as the others. The drawing-room window opened, and from it emerged Mrs. Raycie, in a ruffled sarsenet dress and Point de Paris cap, followed by her two daughters in starched organdy with pink spencers. Mr. Raycie looked with proud approval at his womenkind.

"Gentlemen," said Mrs. Raycie, in a perfectly even voice, "supper is on the table, and if you will do Mr. Raycie and myself the favour—"

"The favour, ma'am," said Mr. Ambrose Huzzard, "is on your side, in so amiably inviting us."

Mrs. Raycie curtsied, the gentlemen bowed, and Mr. Raycie said: "Your arm to Mrs. Raycie, Huzzard. This little farewell party is a family affair, and the other gentlemen must content themselves

[20]

with my two daughters. Sarah Anne, Mary Adeline—"

The Commodore and Mr. John Huzzard advanced ceremoniously toward the two girls, and Mr. Kent, being a cousin, closed the procession between Mr. Raycie and Lewis.

Oh, that supper-table! The vision of it used sometimes to rise before Lewis Raycie's eyes in outlandish foreign places; for though not a large or fastidious eater when he was at home, he was afterward, in lands of chestnut-flour and garlic and queer bearded sea-things, to suffer many pangs of hunger at the thought of that opulent board. In the centre stood the Raycie *épergne* of pierced silver, holding aloft a bunch of June roses surrounded by dangling baskets of sugared almonds and striped peppermints; and grouped about this decorative "motif" were Lowestoft platters heavy with piles of raspberries, strawberries and the first Delaware peaches. An outer flanking of heaped-up cookies, crullers, strawberry short-cake, piping hot corn-bread and deep golden butter in moist blocks still bedewed from the muslin swathings of the dairy, led the eye to the Virginia ham in front of Mr. Raycie, and the twin dishes of scrambled eggs on toast and broiled blue-fish over which his wife presided. Lewis could never afterward fit into this intricate pattern the "side-dishes" of devilled turkey-legs and creamed chicken hash, the sliced cucumbers and tomatoes, the heavy silver jugs of butter-coloured cream, the float-ing-island, "slips" and lemon jellies that were somehow interwoven with the solider elements of the design; but they were all there, either together or successively, and so were the towering piles of waffles reeling on their foundations, and the slender silver jugs of maple syrup perpetually escorting them about the table as black Dinah replenished the supply.

They ate—oh, how they all ate!— though the ladies were supposed only to nibble; but the good things on Lewis's plate remained untouched until, ever and again, an admonishing glance from Mr. Raycie, or an entreating one from Mary Adeline, made him insert a languid fork into the heap.

And all the while Mr. Raycie continued to hold forth.

"A young man, in my opinion, before setting up for himself, must see the world; form his taste; fortify his judgment. He must study the most famous monuments, examine the organization of foreign societies, and the habits and customs of those older civilizations whose yoke it has been our glory to cast off. Though he may see in them much to deplore and to reprove—" ("Some of the gals, though," Commodore Ledgely was heard to interject)—"much that will make him give thanks for the privilege of having been born and brought up under our own Free Institutions, yet I believe he will also"— Mr. Raycie conceded it with magnanimity—"be able to learn much."

"The Sundays, though," Mr. Kent hazarded warningly; and Mrs. Raycie breathed across to her son: "Ah, that's what *I* say!"

Mr. Raycie did not like interruption; and he met it by growing visibly larger. His huge bulk hung a moment, like an avalanche, above the silence which followed Mr. Kent's interjection and Mrs. Raycie's murmur; then he crashed down on both.

[24]

"The Sundays—the Sundays? Well, what of the Sundays? What is there to frighten a good Episcopalian in what we call the Continental Sunday? I presume that we're all Churchmen here, eh? No puling Methodists or atheistical Unitarians at my table tonight, that I'm aware of? Nor will I offend the ladies of my household by assuming that they have secretly lent an ear to the Baptist ranter in the chapel at the foot of our lane. No? I thought not! Well, then, I say, what's all this flutter about the Papists? Far be it from me to approve of their heathenish doctrines—but, damn it, they go to church, don't they? And they have a real service, as we do, don't they? And real clergy, and not a lot of nondescripts dressed like laymen, and damned badly at that, who chat familiarly with the Almighty in their own vulgar lingo? No,

sir"—he swung about on the shrinking
Mr. Kent—"it's not the Church I'm
afraid of in foreign countries, it's the
sewers, sir!"

Mrs. Raycie had grown very pale:
Lewis knew that she too was deeply per-
turbed about the sewers. "And the night-
air," she scarce-audibly sighed.

But Mr. Raycie had taken up his main
theme again. "In my opinion, if a young
man travels at all, he must travel as extensively as his—er—means permit; must
see as much of the world as he can. Those
are my son's sailing orders, Commodore;
and here's to his carrying them out to the
best of his powers!"

Black Dinah, removing the Virginia
ham, or rather such of its bony structure
as alone remained on the dish, had managed to make room for a bowl of punch
from which Mr. Raycie poured deep

[26]

ladlefuls of perfumed fire into the glasses ranged before him on a silver tray. The gentlemen rose, the ladies smiled and wept, and Lewis's health and the success of the Grand Tour were toasted with an eloquence which caused Mrs. Raycie, with a hasty nod to her daughters, and a covering rustle of starched flounces, to shepherd them softly from the room.

"After all," Lewis heard her murmur to them on the threshold, "your father's using such language shows that he's in the best of humour with dear Lewis."

II

IN spite of his enforced potations, Lewis Raycie was up the next morning before sunrise.

Unlatching his shutters without noise, he looked forth over the wet lawn merged in a blur of shrubberies, and the waters of the Sound dimly seen beneath a sky full of stars. His head ached but his heart glowed; what was before him was thrilling enough to clear a heavier brain than his.

He dressed quickly and completely (save for his shoes), and then, stripping the flowered quilt from his high mahogany bed, rolled it in a tight bundle under his arm. Thus enigmatically equipped he was feeling his way, shoes in hand, through the darkness of the upper story to the slippery oak stairs, when he was startled by a candle-gleam in the pitch-blackness of the hall below. He held his breath, and leaning over the stair-rail saw with amazement his sister Mary Adeline come forth, cloaked and bonneted, but also in stocking-feet, from the passage leading to the pantry. She too carried a double burden: her shoes and the candle in one hand, in the other a large covered basket that weighed down her bare arm.

Brother and sister stopped and stared at each other in the blue dusk: the upward slant of the candle-light distorted Mary Adeline's mild features, twisting them into a frightened grin as Lewis stole down to join her.

"Oh—" she whispered. "What in the world are you doing here? I was just getting together a few things for that poor young Mrs. Poe down the lane, who's so ill—before mother goes to the store-room. You won't tell, will you?"

Lewis signalled his complicity, and cautiously slid open the bolt of the front door. They durst not say more till they were out of ear-shot. On the doorstep they sat down to put on their shoes; then they hastened on without a word through the ghostly shrubberies till they reached the gate into the lane.

"But you, Lewis?" the sister suddenly questioned, with an astonished stare at the rolled-up quilt under her brother's arm.

"Oh, I—. Look here, Addy—" he broke off and began to grope in his pocket —"I haven't much about me . . . the old gentleman keeps me as close as ever . . . but here's a dollar, if you think that poor Mrs. Poe could use it. . . I'd be too

[30]

happy . . . consider it a privilege. . . "

"Oh, Lewis, Lewis, how noble, how generous of you! Of course I can buy a few extra things with it . . . they never see meat unless I can bring them a bit, you know . . . and I fear she's dying of a decline . . . and she and her mother are so fiery-proud. . . " She wept with gratitude, and Lewis drew a breath of relief. He had diverted her attention from the bed-quilt.

"Ah, there's the breeze," he murmured, sniffing the suddenly chilled air.

"Yes; I must be off; I must be back before the sun is up," said Mary Adeline anxiously, "and it would never do if mother knew—"

"She doesn't know of your visits to Mrs. Poe?"

A look of childish guile sharpened Mary Adeline's undeveloped face. "She

does, of course; but yet she doesn't . . .
we've arranged it so. You see, Mr. Poe's
an Atheist; and so father—"

"I see," Lewis nodded. "Well, we part
here; I'm off for a swim," he said glibly.
But abruptly he turned back and caught
his sister's arm. "Sister, tell Mrs. Poe,
please, that I heard her husband give a
reading from his poems in New York two
nights ago—"

("Oh, Lewis—*you?* But father says
he's a blasphemer!")

"—And that he's a great poet—a Great
Poet. Tell her that from me, will you,
please, Mary Adeline?"

"Oh, brother, I couldn't . . . we never
speak of him," the startled girl faltered,
hurrying away.

In the cove where the Commodore's
sloop had ridden a few hours earlier a big-
gish rowing-boat took the waking ripples.

Young Raycie paddled out to her, fastened his skiff to the moorings, and hastily clambered into the boat.

From various recesses of his pockets he produced rope, string, a carpet-layer's needle, and other unexpected and incongruous tackle; then, lashing one of the oars across the top of the other, and jamming the latter upright between the forward thwart and the bow, he rigged the flowered bed-quilt on this mast, knotted a rope to the free end of the quilt, and sat down in the stern, one hand on the rudder, the other on his improvised sheet.

Venus, brooding silverly above a line of pale green sky, made a pool of glory in the sea as the dawn-breeze plumped the lover's sail. . .

On the shelving pebbles of another cove, two or three miles down the Sound,

Lewis Raycie lowered his queer sail and beached his boat. A clump of willows on the shingle-edge mysteriously stirred and parted, and Treeshy Kent was in his arms.

The sun was just pushing above a belt of low clouds in the east, spattering them with liquid gold, and Venus blanched as the light spread upward. But under the willows it was still dusk, a watery green dusk in which the secret murmurs of the night were caught.

"Treeshy—Treeshy!" the young man cried, kneeling beside her—and then, a moment later: "My angel, are you sure that no one guesses—?"

The girl gave a faint laugh which screwed up her funny nose. She leaned her head on his shoulder, her round forehead and rough braids pressed against his cheek, her hands in his, breathing quickly and joyfully.

[34]

"I thought I should never get here," Lewis grumbled, "with that ridiculous bed-quilt—and it'll be broad day soon! To think that I was of age yesterday, and must come to you in a boat rigged like a child's toy on a duck-pond! If you knew how it humiliates me—"

"What does it matter, dear, since you're of age now, and your own master?"

"But am I, though? He says so—but it's only on his own terms; only while I do what he wants! You'll see. . . I've a credit of ten thousand dollars . . . ten . . . thou . . . sand . . . d'you hear? . . . placed to my name in a London bank; and not a penny here to bless myself with meanwhile. . . Why, Treeshy darling, why, what's the matter?"

She flung her arms about his neck, and through their innocent kisses he could taste her tears. "What *is* it, Treeshy?" he implored her.

"I . . . oh, I'd forgotten it was to be our last day together till you spoke of London—cruel, cruel!" she reproached him; and through the green twilight of the willows her eyes blazed on him like two stormy stars. No other eyes he knew could express such elemental rage as Treeshy's.

"You little spitfire, you!" he laughed back somewhat chokingly. "Yes, it's our last day—but not for long; at our age two years are not so very long, after all, are they? And when I come back to you I'll come as my own master, independent, free—come to claim you in face of everything and everybody! Think of that, darling, and be brave for my sake . . . brave and patient . . . as I mean to be!" he declared heroically.

[36]

"Oh, but you—you'll see other girls; heaps and heaps of them; in those wicked old countries where they're so lovely. My uncle Kent says the European countries are all wicked, even my own poor Italy . . ."

"But *you,* Treeshy; you'll be seeing cousins Bill and Donald meanwhile—seeing them all day long and every day. And you know you've a weakness for that great hulk of a Bill. Ah, if only I stood six-foot-one in my stockings I'd go with an easier heart, you fickle child!" he tried to banter her.

"Fickle? Fickle? *Me*—oh, Lewis!"

He felt the premonitory sweep of sobs, and his untried courage failed him. It was delicious, in theory, to hold weeping beauty to one's breast, but terribly alarming, he found, in practice. There came a responsive twitching in his throat.

"No, no; firm as adamant, true as steel; that's what we both mean to be, isn't it, *cara?*"

"*Caro,* yes," she sighed, appeased.

"And you'll write to me regularly, Treeshy—long long letters? I may count on that, mayn't I, wherever I am? And they must all be numbered, every one of them, so that I shall know at once if I've missed one; remember!"

"And, Lewis, you'll wear them here?" (She touched his breast.) "Oh, not *all,*" she added, laughing, "for they'd make such a big bundle that you'd soon have a hump in front like Pulcinella—but always at least the last one, just the last one. Promise!"

"Always, I promise—as long as they're kind," he said, still struggling to take a spirited line.

"Oh, Lewis, they will be, as long as yours are—and long long afterward. . . "

Venus failed and vanished in the sun's uprising.

III

THE crucial moment, Lewis had always known, would be not that of his farewell to Treeshy, but of his final interview with his father.

On that everything hung: his immediate future as well as his more distant prospects. As he stole home in the early sunlight, over the dew-drenched grass, he glanced up apprehensively at Mr. Raycie's windows, and thanked his stars that they were still tightly shuttered.

There was no doubt, as Mrs. Raycie said, that her husband's "using language" before ladies showed him to be in high good humour, relaxed and slippered, as it were—a state his family so seldom saw him in that Lewis had sometimes impertinently wondered to what awful descent from the clouds he and his two sisters owed their timorous being.

It was all very well to tell himself, as he often did, that the bulk of the money was his mother's, and that he could turn her round his little finger. What difference did that make? Mr. Raycie, the day after his marriage, had quietly taken over the management of his wife's property, and deducted, from the very moderate allowance he accorded her, all her little personal expenses, even to the postage-stamps she used, and the dollar she put in the plate every Sunday. He called the allowance her "pin-money," since, as he often reminded her, he paid all the household bills himself, so that Mrs. Raycie's quarterly pittance could be entirely devoted, if she chose, to frills and feathers.

"And will be, if you respect my wishes,

my dear," he always added. "I like to
see a handsome figure well set-off, and not
to have our friends imagine, when they
come to dine, that Mrs. Raycie is sick
above-stairs, and I've replaced her by a
poor relation in *allapacca*." In compli-
ance with which Mrs. Raycie, at once flattered and terrified, spent her last penny
in adorning herself and her daughters,
and had to stint their bedroom fires, and
the servants' meals, in order to find a
penny for any private necessity.

Mr. Raycie had long since convinced
his wife that this method of dealing with
her, if not lavish, was suitable, and in fact
"handsome"; when she spoke of the subject to her relations it was with tears of
gratitude for her husband's kindness in
assuming the management of her property. As he managed it exceedingly well,
her hard-headed brothers (glad to have

the responsibility off their hands, and convinced that, if left to herself, she would
have muddled her money away in ill-ad-
vised charities) were disposed to share
her approval of Mr. Raycie; though her
old mother sometimes said helplessly:
"When I think that Lucy Ann can't as
much as have a drop of gruel brought up
to her without his weighing the oat-
meal. . . " But even that was only whispered, lest Mr. Raycie's mysterious fac-
ulty of hearing what was said behind his
back should bring sudden reprisals on the
venerable lady to whom he always alluded,
with a tremor in his genial voice, as "my
dear mother-in-law—unless indeed she
will allow me to call her, more briefly but
more truly, my dear mother."

To Lewis, hitherto, Mr. Raycie had
meted the same measure as to the females
of the household. He had dressed him

well, educated him expensively, lauded him to the skies—and counted every penny of his allowance. Yet there was a difference; and Lewis was as well aware of it as any one.

The dream, the ambition, the passion of Mr. Raycie's life, was (as his son knew) to found a Family; and he had only Lewis to found it with. He believed in primogeniture, in heirlooms, in entailed estates, in all the ritual of the English "landed" tradition. No one was louder than he in praise of the democratic institutions under which he lived; but he never thought of them as affecting that more private but more important institution, the Family; and to the Family all his care and all his thoughts were given. The result, as Lewis dimly guessed, was, that upon his own shrinking and inadequate head was centred all the passion contained

in the vast expanse of Mr. Raycie's
breast. Lewis was his very own, and
Lewis represented what was most dear to
him; and for both these reasons Mr.
Raycie set an inordinate value on the boy
(a quite different thing, Lewis thought
from loving him).

Mr. Raycie was particularly proud of
his son's taste for letters. Himself not a
wholly unread man, he admired intensely
what he called the "cultivated gentleman"
—and that was what Lewis was evidently
going to be. Could he have combined
with this tendency a manlier frame, and
an interest in the few forms of sport then
popular among gentlemen, Mr. Raycie's
satisfaction would have been complete;
but whose is, in this disappointing world?
Meanwhile he flattered himself that,
Lewis being still young and malleable,
and his health certainly mending, two

years of travel and adventure might send him back a very different figure, physically as well as mentally. Mr. Raycie had himself travelled in his youth, and was persuaded that the experience was formative; he secretly hoped for the return of a bronzed and broadened Lewis, seasoned by independence and adventure, and having discreetly sown his wild oats in foreign pastures, where they would not contaminate the home crop.

All this Lewis guessed; and he guessed as well that these two wander-years were intended by Mr. Raycie to lead up to a marriage and an establishment after Mr. Raycie's own heart, but in which Lewis's was not to have even a consulting voice.

"He's going to give me all the advantages—for his own purpose," the young man summed it up as he went down to join the family at the breakfast table.

Mr. Raycie was never more resplendent than at that moment of the day and season. His spotless white duck trousers, strapped under kid boots, his thin kerseymere coat, and drab *piqué* waistcoat crossed below a snowy stock, made him look as fresh as the morning and as appetizing as the peaches and cream banked before him.

Opposite sat Mrs. Raycie, immaculate also, but paler than usual, as became a mother about to part from her only son; and between the two was Sarah Anne, unusually pink, and apparently occupied in trying to screen her sister's empty seat. Lewis greeted them, and seated himself at his mother's right.

Mr. Raycie drew out his *guillochée* repeating watch, and detaching it from its heavy gold chain laid it on the table beside him.

"Mary Adeline is late again. It is a somewhat unusual thing for a sister to be late at the last meal she is to take—for two years—with her only brother."

"Oh, Mr. Raycie!" Mrs. Raycie faltered.

"I say, the idea is peculiar. Perhaps," said Mr. Raycie sarcastically, "I am going to be blessed with a *peculiar* daughter."

"I'm afraid Mary Adeline is beginning a sick headache, sir. She tried to get up, but really could not," said Sarah Anne in a rush.

Mr. Raycie's only reply was to arch ironic eyebrows, and Lewis hastily intervened: "I'm sorry, sir; but it may be my fault—"

Mrs. Raycie paled, Sarah Anne, purpled, and Mr. Raycie echoed with punctilious incredulity: "Your—fault?"

"In being the occasion, sir, of last night's too-sumptuous festivity—"

"Ha—ha—ha!" Mr. Raycie laughed, his thunders instantly dispelled.

He pushed back his chair and nodded to his son with a smile; and the two, leaving the ladies to wash up the teacups (as was still the habit in genteel families) betook themselves to Mr. Raycie's study.

What Mr. Raycie studied in this apartment—except the accounts, and ways of making himself unpleasant to his family—Lewis had never been able to discover. It was a small bare formidable room; and the young man, who never crossed the threshold but with a sinking of his heart, felt it sink lower than ever. *"Now!"* he thought.

Mr. Raycie took the only easy-chair, and began.

"My dear fellow, our time is short, but long enough for what I have to say. In a few hours you will be setting out on your great journey: an important event in the life of any young man. Your talents and character—combined with your means of improving the opportunity—make me hope that in your case it will be decisive. I expect you to come home from this trip a man—"

So far, it was all to order, so to speak; Lewis could have recited it beforehand. He bent his head in acquiescence.

"A man," Mr. Raycie repeated, "prepared to play a part, a considerable part, in the social life of the community. I expect you to be a figure in New York; and I shall give you the means to be so." He cleared his throat. "But means are not enough—though you must never forget that they are essential. Education,

[50]

polish, experience of the world; these are what so many of our men of standing lack. What do they know of Art or Letters? We have had little time here to produce either as yet—you spoke?" Mr. Raycie broke off with a crushing courtesy.

"I—oh, no," his son stammered.

"Ah; I thought you might be about to allude to certain blasphemous penny-a-liners whose poetic ravings are said to have given them a kind of pothouse notoriety."

Lewis reddened at the allusion but was silent, and his father went on:

"Where is our Byron—our Scott—our Shakespeare? And in painting it is the same. Where are our Old Masters? We are not without contemporary talent; but for works of genius we must still look to the past; we must, in most cases, content ourselves with copies. . . Ah, here,

I know, my dear boy, I touch a responsive chord! Your love of the arts has not passed unperceived; and I mean, I desire, to do all I can to encourage it. Your future position in the world—your duties and obligations as a gentleman and a man of fortune—will not permit you to become, yourself, an eminent painter or a famous sculptor; but I shall raise no objection to your dabbling in these arts as an amateur—at least while you are travelling abroad. It will form your taste, strengthen your judgment, and give you, I hope, the discernment necessary to select for me a few masterpieces which shall *not* be copies. Copies," Mr. Raycie pursued with a deepening emphasis, "are for the less discriminating, or for those less blessed with this world's goods. Yes, my dear Lewis, I wish to create a gallery: a gallery of Heirlooms. Your mother participates in this ambition—she desires to see on our walls a few original specimens of the Italian genius. Raphael, I fear, we can hardly aspire to; but a Domenichino, an Albano, a Carlo Dolci, a Guercino, a Carlo Maratta—one or two of Salvator Rosa's noble landscapes . . . you see my idea? There shall be a Raycie Gallery; and it shall be your mission to get together its nucleus." Mr. Raycie paused, and mopped his flowing forehead. "I believe I could have given my son no task more to his liking."

"Oh, no, sir, none indeed!" Lewis cried, flushing and paling. He had in fact never suspected this part of his father's plan, and his heart swelled with the honour of so unforeseen a mission. Nothing, in truth, could have made him prouder or happier. For a moment he forgot love, forgot Treeshy, forgot every-

thing but the rapture of moving among
the masterpieces of which he had so long
dreamed, moving not as a mere hungry
spectator but as one whose privilege it
should at least be to single out and carry
away some of the lesser treasures. He
could hardly take in what had happened,
and the shock of the announcement left
him, as usual, inarticulate.

He heard his father booming on, de-
veloping the plan, explaining with his
usual pompous precision that one of the
partners of the London bank in which
Lewis's funds were deposited was himself a noted collector, and had agreed to
provide the young traveller with letters
of introduction to other connoisseurs, both
in France and Italy, so that Lewis's ac-
quisitions might be made under the most
enlightened guidance.

"It is," Mr. Raycie concluded, "in order

to put you on a footing of equality with
the best collectors that I have placed such
a large sum at your disposal. I reckon
that for ten thousand dollars you can
travel for two years in the very best style;
and I mean to place another five thousand to your credit"—he paused, and let
the syllables drop slowly into his son's
brain: "five thousand dollars for the pur-
chase of works of art, which eventually—
remember—will be yours; and will be
handed on, I trust, to your sons' sons
as long as the name of Raycie survives"—
a length of time, Mr. Raycie's tone
seemed to imply, hardly to be measured
in periods less extensive than those of the
Egyptian dynasties.

Lewis heard him with a whirling brain.
Five thousand dollars! The sum seemed
so enormous, even in dollars, and so in-
calculably larger when translated into any

continental currency, that he wondered why his father, in advance, had given up all hope of a Raphael. . . "If I travel economically," he said to himself, "and deny myself unnecessary luxuries, I may yet be able to surprise him by bringing one back. And my mother—how magnanimous, how splendid! Now I see why she has consented to all the little economies that sometimes seemed so paltry and so humiliating. . ."

The young man's eyes filled with tears, but he was still silent, though he longed as never before to express his gratitude and admiration to his father. He had entered the study expecting a parting sermon on the subject of thrift, coupled with the prospective announcement of a "suitable establishment" (he could even guess the particular Huzzard girl his father had in view) ; and instead he had been told to spend his princely allowance in a princely manner, and to return home with a gallery of masterpieces. "At least," he murmured to himself, "it shall contain a Correggio."

"Well, sir?" Mr. Raycie boomed.

"Oh, sir—" his son cried, and flung himself on the vast slope of the parental waistcoat.

Amid all these accumulated joys there murmured deep down in him the thought that nothing had been said or done to interfere with his secret plans about Treeshy. It seemed almost as if his father had tacitly accepted the idea of their unmentioned engagement; and Lewis felt half guilty at not confessing to it then and there. But the gods are formidable even when they unbend; never more so, perhaps, than at such moments. . .

PART II

IV

LEWIS RAYCIE stood on a projecting rock and surveyed the sublime spectacle of Mont Blanc.

It was a brilliant August day, and the air, at that height, was already so sharp that he had had to put on his fur-lined pelisse. Behind him, at a respectful distance, was the travelling servant who, at a signal, had brought it up to him; below, in the bend of the mountain road, stood the light and elegant carriage which had carried him thus far on his travels.

Scarcely more than a year had passed since he had waved a farewell to New York from the deck of the packet-ship headed down the bay; yet, to the young man confidently facing Mont Blanc, nothing seemed left in him of that fluid and insubstantial being, the former Lewis Raycie, save a lurking and abeyant fear of Mr. Raycie senior. Even that, however, was so attenuated by distance and time, so far sunk below the horizon, and anchored on the far side of the globe, that it stirred in its sleep only when a handsomely folded and wafered letter in his parent's writing was handed out across the desk of some continental counting-house. Mr. Raycie senior did not write often, and when he did it was in a bland and stilted strain. He felt at a disadvantage on paper, and his natural sarcasm was swamped in the rolling periods which it cost him hours of labour to bring forth; so that the dreaded quality lurked for his son only in the curve of certain letters, and in a positively awful way of

[62]

writing out, at full length, the word
Esquire.

It was not that Lewis had broken with
all the memories of his past of a year
ago. Many still lingered in him, or
rather had been transferred to the new
man he had become—as for instance his
tenderness for Treeshy Kent, which,
somewhat to his surprise, had obstinately
resisted all the assaults of English keep-
sake beauties and almond-eyed houris of
the East. It startled him, at times, to
find Treeshy's short dusky face, with its
round forehead, the widely spaced eyes
and the high cheek-bones, starting out at
him suddenly in the street of some legen-
dary town, or in a landscape of languid
beauty, just as he had now and again been
arrested in an exotic garden by the very
scent of the verbena under the verandah
at home. His travels had confirmed

rather than weakened the family view of
Treeshy's plainness; she could not be
made to fit into any of the patterns of
female beauty so far submitted to him;
yet there she was, ensconced in his new
heart and mind as deeply as in the old,
though her kisses seemed less vivid, and
the peculiar rough notes of her voice
hardly reached him. Sometimes, half irritably, he said to himself that with an
effort he could disperse her once for all;
yet she lived on in him, unseen yet in-
effaceable, like the image on a daguerreo-
type plate, no less there because so often
invisible.

To the new Lewis, however, the whole
business was less important than he had
once thought it. His suddenly acquired
maturity made Treeshy seem a petted
child rather than the guide, the Beatrice,
he had once considered her; and he prom-

ised himself, with an elderly smile, that as soon as he got to Italy he would write her the long letter for which he was now considerably in her debt.

His travels had first carried him to England. There he spent some weeks in collecting letters and recommendations for his tour, in purchasing his travelling-carriage and its numerous appurtenances, and in driving in it from cathedral town to storied castle, omitting nothing, from Abbotsford to Kenilworth, which deserved the attention of a cultivated mind. From England he crossed to Calais, moving slowly southward to the Mediterranean; and there, taking ship for the Piræus, he plunged into pure romance, and the tourist became a Giaour.

It was the East which had made him into a new Lewis Raycie; the East, so squalid and splendid, so pestilent and so poetic, so full of knavery and romance and fleas and nightingales, and so different, alike in its glories and its dirt, from what his studious youth had dreamed. After Smyrna and the bazaars, after Damascus and Palmyra, the Acropolis, Mytilene and Sunium, what could be left in his mind of Canal Street and the lawn above the Sound? Even the mosquitoes, which seemed at first the only connecting link, were different, because he fought with them in scenes so different; and a young gentleman who had journeyed across the desert in Arabian dress, slept under goats'-hair tents, been attacked by robbers in the Peloponnesus and despoiled by his own escort at Baalbek, and by customs' officials everywhere, could not but look with a smile on the terrors that walk New York and the Hudson river. Encased in security and monotony, that

[66]

other Lewis Raycie, when his little figure bobbed up to the surface, seemed like a new-born babe preserved in alcohol. Even Mr. Raycie senior's thunders were now no more than the far-off murmur of summer lightning on a perfect evening. Had Mr. Raycie ever really frightened Lewis? Why, now he was not even frightened by Mont Blanc!

He was still gazing with a sense of easy equality at its awful pinnacles when another travelling-carriage paused near his own, and a young man, eagerly jumping from it, and also followed by a servant with a cloak, began to mount the slope. Lewis at once recognized the carriage, and the light springing figure of the young man, his blue coat and swelling stock, and the scar slightly distorting his handsome and eloquent mouth. It was the Englishman who had arrived at

the Montanvert inn the night before with
a valet, a guide, and such a cargo of books,
maps and sketching-materials as threat-
ened to overshadow even Lewis's outfit.

Lewis, at first, had not been greatly
drawn to the newcomer, who, seated aloof
in the dining-room, seemed not to see his
fellow-traveller. The truth was that Lewis
was dying for a little conversation. His
astonishing experiences were so tightly
packed in him (with no outlet save the
meagre trickle of his nightly diary) that
he felt they would soon melt into the
vague blur of other people's travels unless he could give them fresh reality by
talking them over. And the stranger
with the deep-blue eyes that matched his
coat, the scarred cheek and eloquent lip,
seemed to Lewis a worthy listener. The
Englishman appeared to think otherwise.
He preserved an air of moody abstraction,

which Lewis's vanity imagined him to
have put on as the gods becloud themselves for their secret errands; and the
curtness of his goodnight was (Lewis
flattered himself) surpassed only by the
young New Yorker's.

But today all was different. The
stranger advanced affably, raised his hat
from his tossed statue-like hair, and en-
quired with a smile: "Are you by any
chance interested in the forms of cirrous
clouds?"

His voice was as sweet as his smile, and
the two were reinforced by a glance so
winning that it made the odd question
seem not only pertinent but natural.
Lewis, though surprised, was not discon-
certed. He merely coloured with the
unwonted sense of his ignorance, and replied ingenuously: "I believe, sir, I am
interested in everything."

"A noble answer!" cried the other, and held out his hand.

"But I must add," Lewis continued with courageous honesty, "that I have never as yet had occasion to occupy myself particularly with the forms of cirrous clouds."

His companion looked at him merrily. "That," said he, "is no reason why you shouldn't begin to do so now!" To which Lewis as merrily agreed. "For in order to be interested in things," the other continued more gravely, "it is only necessary to see them; and I believe I am not wrong in saying that you are one of the privileged beings to whom the seeing eye has been given."

Lewis blushed his agreement, and his interlocutor continued: "You are one of those who have been on the road to Damascus."

"On the road? I've been to the place itself!" the wanderer exclaimed, bursting with the particulars of his travels; and then blushed more deeply at the perception that the other's use of the name had of course been figurative.

The young Englishman's face lit up. "You've been to Damascus—literally been there yourself? But that may be almost as interesting, in its quite different way, as the formation of clouds or lichens. For the present," he continued with a gesture toward the mountain, "I must devote myself to the extremely inadequate rendering of some of these delicate *aiguilles;* a bit of drudgery not likely to interest you in the face of so sublime a scene. But perhaps this evening—if, as I think, we are staying in the same inn—you will give me a few minutes of your society, and tell me something of your travels. My father," he added with his engaging smile, "has had packed with my paint-brushes a few bottles of a wholly trustworthy Madeira; and if you will favour me with your company at dinner. . . "

He signed to his servant to undo the sketching materials, spread his cloak on the rock, and was already lost in his task as Lewis descended to the carriage.

The Madeira proved as trustworthy as his host had promised. Perhaps it was its exceptional quality which threw such a golden lustre over the dinner; unless it were rather the conversation of the blue-eyed Englishman which made Lewis Raycie, always a small drinker, feel that in his company every drop was nectar.

When Lewis joined his host it had been with the secret hope of at last being able to talk; but when the evening was over (and they kept it up to the small hours) he perceived that he had chiefly listened. Yet there had been no sense of suppression, of thwarted volubility; he had been given all the openings he wanted. Only, whenever he produced a little fact it was instantly overflowed by the other's imagination till it burned like a dull pebble tossed into a rushing stream. For whatever Lewis said was seen by his companion from a new angle, and suggested a new train of thought; each commonplace item of experience became a many-faceted crystal flashing with unexpected fires. The young Englishman's mind moved in a world of associations and references far more richly peopled than Lewis's; but his eager communicativeness, his directness of speech and manner, instantly opened its gates to the simpler youth. It was certainly not the Madeira which sped the hours and flooded them with magic; but the magic gave the Madeira—excellent, and reputed of its kind, as Lewis afterward learned—a taste no other vintage was to have for him.

"Oh, but we must meet again in Italy— there are many things there that I could perhaps help you to see," the young Englishman declared as they swore eternal friendship on the stairs of the sleeping inn.

V

IT was in a tiny Venetian church, no
more than a chapel, that Lewis
Raycie's eyes had been unsealed—in a
dull-looking little church not even men-
tioned in the guide-books. But for his
chance encounter with the young Englishman in the shadow of Mont Blanc,
Lewis would never have heard of the
place; but then what else that was worth
knowing would he ever have heard of, he
wondered?

He had stood a long time looking at
the frescoes, put off at first—he could
admit it now—by a certain stiffness in the
attitudes of the people, by the childish
elaboration of their dress (so different

from the noble draperies which Sir Joshua's Discourses on Art had taught him to admire in the great painters), and by the innocent inexpressive look in their young faces—for even the gray-beards seemed young. And then suddenly his gaze had lit on one of these faces in particular: that of a girl with round cheeks, high cheek-bones and widely set eyes under an intricate head-dress of pearl-woven braids. Why, it was Treeshy— Treeshy Kent to the life! And so far from being thought "plain," the young lady was no other than the peerless princess about whom the tale revolved. And what a fairy-land she lived in—full of lithe youths and round-faced pouting maidens, rosy old men and burnished blackamoors, pretty birds and cats and nibbling rabbits—and all involved and enclosed in golden balustrades, in colonnades

of pink and blue, laurel-garlands fes-
tooned from ivory balconies, and domes
and minarets against summer seas! Lewis's
imagination lost itself in the scene; he
forgot to regret the noble draperies, the
exalted sentiments, the fuliginous back-
grounds, of the artists he had come to
Italy to admire—forgot Sassoferrato,
Guido Reni, Carlo Dolce, Lo Spagnoletto, the Carracci, and even the Transfig-
uration of Raphael, though he knew it to
be the greatest picture in the world.

After that he had seen almost everything else that Italian art had to offer;
had been to Florence, Naples, Rome; to
Bologna to study the Eclectic School, to
Parma to examine the Correggios and the
Giulio Romanos. But that first vision
had laid a magic seed between his lips;
the seed that makes you hear what the
birds say and the grasses whisper. Even

if his English friend had not continued at his side, pointing out, explaining, inspiring, Lewis Raycie flattered himself that the round face of the little Saint Ursula would have led him safely and confidently past all her rivals. She had become his touchstone, his star: how insipid seemed to him all the sheep-faced Virgins draped in red and blue paint after he had looked into her wondering girlish eyes and traced the elaborate pattern of her brocades! He could remember now, quite distinctly, the day when he had given up even Beatrice Cenci . . . and as for that fat naked Magdalen of Carlo Dolce's, lolling over the book she was not reading, and ogling the spectator in the good old way . . . faugh! Saint Ursula did not need to rescue him from *her*. . .

His eyes had been opened to a new world of art. And this world it was his

mission to reveal to others—he, the insig-
nificant and ignorant Lewis Raycie, as
"but for the grace of God," and that
chance encounter on Mont Blanc, he
might have gone on being to the end!
He shuddered to think of the army of
Neapolitan beggar-boys, bituminous
monks, whirling prophets, languishing
Madonnas and pink-rumped *amorini* who
might have been travelling home with him
in the hold of the fast new steam-
packet.

His excitement had something of the
apostle's ecstasy. He was not only, in a
few hours, to embrace Treeshy, and be
reunited to his honoured parents; he was
also to go forth and preach the new gospel
to them that sat in the darkness of Salvator Rosa and Lo Spagnoletto...

The first thing that struck Lewis was

the smallness of the house on the Sound, and the largeness of Mr. Raycie.

He had expected to receive the opposite impression. In his recollection the varnished Tuscan villa had retained something of its impressiveness, even when compared to its supposed originals. Perhaps the very contrast between their draughty distances and naked floors, and the expensive carpets and bright fires of High Point, magnified his memory of the latter—there were moments when the thought of its groaning board certainly added to the effect. But the image of Mr. Raycie had meanwhile dwindled. Everything about him, as his son looked back, seemed narrow, juvenile, almost childish. His bluster about Edgar Poe, for instance—true poet still to Lewis, though he had since heard richer notes; his fussy tyranny of his womenkind; his un-

conscious but total ignorance of most of
the things, books, people, ideas, that now
filled his son's mind; above all, the arro-
gance and incompetence of his artistic
judgments. Beyond a narrow range of
reading—mostly, Lewis suspected, culled
in drowsy after-dinner snatches from
Knight's "Half-hours with the Best
Authors"—Mr. Raycie made no pretence
to book-learning; left *that,* as he handsomely said, "to the professors." But on
matters of art he was dogmatic and explicit, prepared to justify his opinions by
the citing of eminent authorities and of
market-prices, and quite clear, as his farewell talk with his son had shown, as to
which Old Masters should be privileged
to figure in the Raycie collection.

The young man felt no impatience of
these judgments. America was a long
way from Europe, and it was many years

since Mr. Raycie had travelled. He could hardly be blamed for not knowing that the things he admired were no longer admirable, still less for not knowing why. The pictures before which Lewis had knelt in spirit had been virtually undiscovered, even by art-students and critics, in his father's youth. How was an American gentleman, filled with his own self-importance, and paying his courier the highest salary to show him the accredited "Masterpieces"—how was he to guess that whenever he stood rapt before a Sassoferrato or a Carlo Dolce one of those unknown treasures lurked near by under dust and cobwebs?

No; Lewis felt only tolerance and understanding. Such a view was not one to magnify the paternal image; but when the young man entered the study where Mr. Raycie sat immobilized by gout, the

swathed leg stretched along his sofa
seemed only another reason for indul-
gence ...

Perhaps, Lewis thought afterward, it
was his father's prone position, the way
his great bulk billowed over the sofa, and
the lame leg reached out like a mountain-
ridge, that made him suddenly seem to
fill the room; or else the sound of his voice
booming irritably across the threshold, and
scattering Mrs. Raycie and the girls with
a fierce: "And now, ladies, if the hugging
and kissing are over, I should be glad of
a moment with my son." But it was odd
that, after mother and daughters had
withdrawn with all their hoops and
flounces, the study seemed to grow even
smaller, and Lewis himself to feel more
like a David without the pebble.

"Well, my boy," his father cried, crim-
son and puffing, "here you are at home

again, with many adventures to relate, no doubt; and a few masterpieces to show me, as I gather from the drafts on my exchequer."

"Oh, as to the masterpieces, sir, certainly," Lewis simpered, wondering why his voice sounded so fluty, and his smile was produced with such a conscious muscular effort.

"Good—good," Mr. Raycie approved, waving a violet hand which seemed to be ripening for a bandage. "Reedy carried out my orders, I presume? Saw to it that the paintings were deposited with the bulk of your luggage in Canal Street?"

"Oh, yes, sir; Mr. Reedy was on the dock with precise instructions. You know he always carries out your orders," Lewis ventured with a faint irony.

Mr. Raycie stared. "Mr. Reedy," he said, "does what I tell him, if that's what you mean; otherwise he would hardly have been in my employ for over thirty years."

Lewis was silent, and his father examined him critically. "You appear to have filled out; your health is satisfactory? Well . . . well . . . Mr. Robert Huzzard and his daughters are dining here this evening, by the way, and will no doubt be expecting to see the latest French novelties in stocks and waistcoats. Malvina has become a very elegant figure, your sisters tell me." Mr. Raycie chuckled, and Lewis thought: "I *knew* it was the oldest Huzzard girl!" while a slight chill ran down his spine.

"As to the pictures," Mr. Raycie pursued with growing animation, "I am laid low, as you see, by this cursèd affliction, and till the doctors get me up again, here must I lie and try to imagine how your treasures will look in the new gallery.

And meanwhile, my dear boy, I need hardly say that no one is to be admitted to see them till they have been inspected by me and suitably hung. Reedy shall begin unpacking at once; and when we move to town next month Mrs. Raycie, God willing, shall give the handsomest evening party New York has yet seen, to show my son's collection, and perhaps . . . eh, well? . . . to celebrate another interesting event in his history."

Lewis met this with a faint but respectful gurgle, and before his blurred eyes rose the wistful face of Treeshy Kent.

"Ah, well, I shall see her tomorrow," he thought, taking heart again as soon as he was out of his father's presence.

VI

MR. RAYCIE stood silent for a long time after making the round of the room in the Canal Street house where the unpacked pictures had been set out.

He had driven to town alone with Lewis, sternly rebuffing his daughters' timid hints, and Mrs. Raycie's mute but visible yearning to accompany him. Though the gout was over he was still weak and irritable, and Mrs. Raycie, fluttered at the thought of "crossing him," had swept the girls away at his first frown.

Lewis's hopes rose as he followed his parent's limping progress. The pictures, though standing on chairs and tables, and set clumsily askew to catch the light, bloomed out of the half-dusk of the empty house with a new and persuasive beauty. Ah, how right he had been—how inevitable that his father should own it!

Mr. Raycie halted in the middle of the room. He was still silent, and his face, so quick to frown and glare, wore the calm, almost expressionless look known to Lewis as the mask of inward perplexity. "Oh, of course it will take a little time," the son thought, tingling with the eagerness of youth.

At last, Mr. Raycie woke the echoes by clearing his throat; but the voice which issued from it was as inexpressive as his face. "It is singular," he said, "how little the best copies of the Old Masters resemble the originals. For these *are* Originals?" he questioned, suddenly swinging about on Lewis.

"Oh, absolutely, sir! Besides—" The

young man was about to add: "No one would ever have taken the trouble to copy them"—but hastily checked himself.

"Besides——?"

"I meant, I had the most competent advice obtainable."

"So I assume; since it was the express condition on which I authorized your purchases."

Lewis felt himself shrinking and his father expanding; but he sent a glance along the wall, and beauty shed her reviving beam on him.

Mr. Raycie's brows projected ominously; but his face remained smooth and dubious. Once more he cast a slow glance about him.

"Let us," he said pleasantly, "begin with the Raphael." And it was evident that he did not know which way to turn.

"Oh, sir, a Raphael nowadays—I

warned you it would be far beyond my
budget."

Mr. Raycie's face fell slightly. "I had
hoped nevertheless . . . for an inferior
specimen. . . " Then, with an effort:
"The Sassoferrato, then."

Lewis felt more at his ease; he even
ventured a respectful smile. "Sassoferrato is *all* inferior, isn't he? The fact is,
he no longer stands . . . quite as he used
to. . ."

Mr. Raycie stood motionless: his eyes
were vacuously fixed on the nearest picture.

"Sassoferrato . . . no longer . . . ?"

"Well, sir, *no;* not for a collection of
this quality."

Lewis saw that he had at last struck
the right note. Something large and un-
comfortable appeared to struggle in Mr.
Raycie's throat; then he gave a cough

which might almost have been said to cast out Sassoferrato.

There was another pause before he pointed with his stick to a small picture representing a snub-nosed young woman with a high forehead and jewelled coif, against a background of delicately interwoven columbines. "Is *that*," he questioned, "your Carlo Dolce? The style is much the same, I see; but it seems to me lacking in his peculiar sentiment."

"Oh, but it's not a Carlo Dolce: it's a Piero della Francesca, sir!" burst in triumph from the trembling Lewis.

His father sternly faced him. "It's a *copy,* you mean? I thought so!"

"No, no; not a copy; it's by a great painter . . . a much greater . . ."

Mr. Raycie had reddened sharply at his mistake. To conceal his natural annoyance he assumed a still more silken manner. "In that case," he said, "I think I should like to see the inferior painters first. Where *is* the Carlo Dolce?"

"There *is* no Carlo Dolce," said Lewis, white to the lips.

The young man's next distinct recollection was of standing, he knew not how long afterward, before the armchair in which his father had sunk down, almost as white and shaken as himself.

"This," stammered Mr. Raycie, "this is going to bring back my gout..." But when Lewis entreated: "Oh, sir, do let us drive back quietly to the country, and give me a chance later to explain . . . to put my case" . . . the old gentleman had struck through the pleading with a furious wave of his stick.

"Explain later? Put your case later? It's just what I insist upon your doing

here and now!" And Mr. Raycie added
hoarsely, and as if in actual physical
anguish: "I understand that young John
Huzzard returned from Rome last week
with a Raphael."

After that, Lewis heard himself—as if
with the icy detachment of a spectator—
marshalling his arguments, pleading the
cause he hoped his pictures would have
pleaded for him, dethroning the old Powers and Principalities, and setting up these
new names in their place. It was first
of all the names that stuck in Mr. Raycie's throat: after spending a life-time in
committing to memory the correct pro-
nunciation of words like Lo Spagnoletto
and Giulio Romano, it was bad enough,
his wrathful eyes seemed to say, to have
to begin a new set of verbal gymnastics
before you could be sure of saying to a

friend with careless accuracy: "And *this* is my Giotto da Bondone."

But that was only the first shock, soon forgotten in the rush of greater tribulation. For one might conceivably learn how to pronounce Giotto da Bondone, and even enjoy doing so, provided the friend in question recognized the name and bowed to its authority. But to have your effort received by a blank stare, and the playful request: "You'll have to say that over again, please"—to know that, in going the round of the gallery (the Raycie Gallery!) the same stare and the same request were likely to be repeated before each picture; the bitterness of this was so great that Mr. Raycie, without exaggeration, might have likened his case to that of Agag.

"God! God! God! Carpatcher, you say this other fellow's called? Kept him

back till the last because it's the gem of
the collection, did you? Carpatcher—
well, he'd have done better to stick to his
trade. Something to do with those new
European steam-cars, I suppose, eh?" Mr.
Raycie was so incensed that his irony was
less subtle than usual. "And Angelico
you say did that kind of Noah's Ark sol-
dier in pink armour on gold-leaf? Well,
there I've caught you tripping, my boy.
Not Angelic*o*, Angelic*a;* Angelica Kauff-
man was a lady. And the damned swindler
who foisted that barbarous daub on
you as a picture of hers deserves to be
drawn and quartered—and shall be, sir,
by God, if the law can reach him! He
shall disgorge every penny he's rooked
you out of, or my name's not Halston
Raycie! A bargain . . . you say the
thing was a *bargain?* Why, the price of
a clean postage stamp would be too dear

for it! God—my son; do you realize you had a *trust* to carry out?"

"Yes, sir, yes; and it's just because—"

"You might have written; you might at least have placed your views before me ..."

How could Lewis say: "If I had, I knew you'd have refused to let me buy the pictures?" He could only stammer: "I *did* allude to the revolution in taste ... new names coming up ... you may remember ..."

"Revolution! New names! Who says so? I had a letter last week from the London dealers to whom I especially recommended you, telling me that an undoubted Guido Reni was coming into the market this summer."

"Oh, the dealers—*they* don't know!"

"The dealers ... don't? ... Who does ... except yourself?" Mr. Raycie pronounced in a white sneer.

Lewis, as white, still held his ground. "I wrote you, sir, about my friends; in Italy, and afterward in England."

"Well, God damn it, I never heard of one of *their* names before, either; no more'n of these painters of yours here. I supplied you with the names of all the advisers you needed, and all the painters, too; I all but made the collection for you myself, before you started. . . I was explicit enough, in all conscience, wasn't I?"

Lewis smiled faintly. "That's what I hoped the pictures would be . . ."

"What? Be what? What'd you mean?"

"Be explicit. . . Speak for themselves . . . make you see that their painters are already superseding some of the better-known . . ."

Mr. Raycie gave an awful laugh. "They are, are they?" In whose estimation? Your friends', I suppose. What's the name, again, of that fellow you met in Italy, who picked 'em out for you?"

"Ruskin—John Ruskin," said Lewis.

Mr. Raycie's laugh, prolonged, gathered up into itself a fresh shower of expletives. "Ruskin—Ruskin—just plain John Ruskin, eh? And who *is* this great John Ruskin, who sets God A'mighty right in his judgments? Who'd you say John Ruskin's father was, now?"

"A respected wine-merchant in London, sir."

Mr. Raycie ceased to laugh: he looked at his son with an expression of unutterable disgust.

"Retail?"

"I . . . believe so . . ."

"Faugh!" said Mr. Raycie.

"It wasn't only Ruskin, father. . . . I told you of those other friends in London, whom I met on the way home. They inspected the pictures, and all of them agreed that . . . that the collection would some day be very valuable."

"*Some day*—did they give you a date . . . the month and the year? Ah, those other friends; yes. You said there was a Mr. Brown and a Mr. Hunt and a Mr. Rossiter, was it? Well, I never heard of any of those names, either—except perhaps in a trades' directory."

"It's not Rossiter, father: Dante Rossetti."

"Excuse me: Rossetti. And what does Mr. Dante Rossetti's father do? Sell macaroni, I presume?"

Lewis was silent, and Mr. Raycie went on, speaking now with a deadly steadiness: "The friends I sent you to were judges of art, sir; men who know what a picture's worth; not one of 'em but

could pick out a genuine Raphael.
Couldn't you find 'em when you got to
England? Or hadn't they the time to
spare for you? You'd better not," Mr.
Raycie added, "tell me *that,* for I know
how they'd have received your father's
son."

"Oh, most kindly . . . they did indeed,
sir . . ."

"Ay; but that didn't suit you. You
didn't *want* to be advised. You wanted to
show off before a lot of ignoramuses like
yourself. You wanted—how'd I know
what you wanted? It's as if I'd never
given you an instruction or laid a charge
on you! And the money—God! Where'd
it go to? Buying *this?* Nonsense—."
Mr. Raycie raised himself heavily on his
stick and fixed his angry eyes on his son.
"Own up, Lewis; tell me they got it out
of you at cards. Professional gamblers

the lot, I make no doubt; your Ruskin
and your Morris and your Rossiter.
Make a business to pick up young American greenhorns on their travels, I dare-
say... No? Not that, you say? Then—
women? . . . God A'mighty, Lewis,"
gasped Mr. Raycie, tottering toward his
son with outstretched stick, "I'm no blue-
nosed Puritan, sir, and I'd a damn sight
rather you told me you'd spent it on a
woman, every penny of it, than let yourself be fleeced like a simpleton, buying
these things that look more like cuts out
o' Foxe's Book of Martyrs than Originals
of the Old Masters for a Gentleman's
Gallery... Youth's youth... Gad, sir,
I've been young myself . . . a fellow's got
to go through his apprenticeship. . .
Own up now: women?"

"Oh, not women——"

"Not even!" Mr. Raycie groaned. "All

in pictures, then? Well, say no more to me now. . . I'll get home, I'll get home. . . " He cast a last apoplectic glance about the room. "The Raycie Gallery! That pack of bones and mummers' finery! . . . Why, let alone the rest, there's not a full-bodied female among 'em. . . Do you know what those Madonnas of yours are like, my son? Why, there ain't one of 'em that don't remind me of a bad likeness of poor Treeshy Kent. . . I should say you'd hired half the sign-painters of Europe to do her portrait for you—if I could imagine your wanting it. . . No, sir! I don't need your arm," Mr Raycie snarled, heaving his great bulk painfully across the hall. He withered Lewis with a last look from the doorstep. "And to buy *that* you overdrew your account?—No, I'll drive home alone."

VII

MR. RAYCIE did not die till nearly
a year later; but New York agreed
it was the affair of the pictures that had
killed him.

The day after his first and only sight
of them he sent for his lawyer, and it
became known that he had made a new
will. Then he took to his bed with a return of the gout, and grew so rapidly
worse that it was thought "only proper"
to postpone the party Mrs. Raycie was
to have given that autumn to inaugurate
the gallery. This enabled the family to
pass over in silence the question of the
works of art themselves; but outside of the
Raycie house, where they were never men-

tioned, they formed, that winter, a frequent and fruitful topic of discussion.

Only two persons besides Mr. Raycie were known to have seen them. One was Mr. Donaldson Kent, who owed the privilege to the fact of having once been to Italy; the other, Mr. Reedy, the agent, who had unpacked the pictures. Mr. Reedy, beset by Raycie cousins and old family friends, had replied with genuine humility: "Why, the truth is, I never was taught to see any difference between one picture and another, except as regards the size of them; and these struck me as smallish . . . on the small side, I would say. . . "

Mr. Kent was known to have unbosomed himself to Mr. Raycie with considerable frankness—he went so far, it was rumoured, as to declare that he had never seen any pictures in Italy like those brought back by Lewis, and begged to doubt if they really came from there. But in public he maintained that noncommittal attitude which passed for prudence, but proceeded only from timidity; no one ever got anything from him but the guarded statement: "The subjects are wholly inoffensive."

It was believed that Mr. Raycie dared not consult the Huzzards. Young John Huzzard had just brought home a Raphael; it would have been hard not to avoid comparisons which would have been too galling. Neither to them, nor to any one else, did Mr. Raycie ever again allude to the Raycie Gallery. But when his will was opened it was found that he had bequeathed the pictures to his son. The rest of his property was left absolutely to his two daughters. The bulk of the estate was Mrs. Raycie's; but it was known that

Mrs. Raycie had had her instructions, and among them, perhaps, was the order to fade away in her turn after six months of widowhood. When she had been laid beside her husband in Trinity church-yard her will (made in the same week as Mr. Raycie's, and obviously at his dictation) was found to allow five thousand dollars a year to Lewis during his life-time; the residue of the fortune, which Mr. Raycie's thrift and good management had made into one of the largest in New York, was divided between the daughters. Of these, the one promptly married a Kent and the other a Huzzard; and the latter, Sarah Ann (who had never been Lewis's favourite), was wont to say in later years: "Oh, no, I never grudged my poor brother those funny old pictures. You see, we have a Raphael."

The house stood on the corner of Third
Avenue and Tenth Street. It had lately
come to Lewis Raycie as his share in the
property of a distant cousin, who had
made an "old New York will" under
which all his kin benefited in proportion
to their consanguinity. The neighbour-
hood was unfashionable, and the house in
bad repair; but Mr. and Mrs. Lewis Raycie, who, since their marriage, had been
living in retirement at Tarrytown, im-
mediately moved into it.

Their arrival excited small attention.
Within a year of his father's death, Lewis
had married Treeshy Kent. The alliance
had not been encouraged by Mr. and Mrs.
Kent, who went so far as to say that their
niece might have done better; but as that
one of their sons who was still unmarried
had always shown a lively sympathy for
Treeshy, they yielded to the prudent

thought that, after all, it was better than having her entangle Bill.

The Lewis Raycies had been four years married, and during that time had dropped out of the memory of New York as completely as if their exile had covered half a century. Neither of them had ever cut a great figure there. Treeshy had been nothing but the Kents' Cinderella, and Lewis's ephemeral importance, as heir to the Raycie millions, had been effaced by the painful episode which resulted in his being deprived of them.

So secluded was their way of living, and so much had it come to be a habit, that when Lewis announced that he had inherited Uncle Ebenezer's house his wife hardly looked up from the baby-blanket she was embroidering.

"Uncle Ebenezer's house in New York?"

He drew a deep breath. "Now I shall be able to show the pictures."

"Oh, Lewis—" She dropped the blanket. "Are we going to live there?"

"Certainly. But the house is so large that I shall turn the two corner rooms on the ground floor into a gallery. They are very suitably lighted. It was there that Cousin Ebenezer was laid out."

"Oh, Lewis——"

If anything could have made Lewis Raycie believe in his own strength of will it was his wife's attitude. Merely to hear that unquestioning murmur of submission was to feel something of his father's tyrannous strength arise in him; but with the wish to use it more humanely.

"You'll like that, Treeshy? It's been dull for you here, I know."

She flushed up. "Dull? With *you,*

darling? Besides, I like the country. But I shall like Tenth Street too. Only—you said there were repairs?"

He nodded sternly. "I shall borrow money to make them. If necessary—" he lowered his voice—"I shall mortgage the pictures."

He saw her eyes fill. "Oh, but it won't be! There are so many ways still in which I can economize."

He laid his hand on hers and turned his profile toward her, because he knew it was so much stronger than his full face. He did not feel sure that she quite grasped his intention about the pictures; was not even certain that he wished her to. He went in to New York every week now, occupying himself mysteriously and importantly with plans, specifications and other business transactions with long names; while Treeshy, through the hot summer months, sat in Tarrytown and waited for the baby.

A little girl was born at the end of the summer and christened Louisa; and when she was a few weeks old the Lewis Raycies left the country for New York.

"Now!" thought Lewis, as they bumped over the cobblestones of Tenth Street in the direction of Cousin Ebenezer's house.

The carriage stopped, he handed out his wife, the nurse followed with the baby, and they all stood and looked up at the house-front.

"Oh, Lewis—" Treeshy gasped; and even little Louisa set up a sympathetic wail.

Over the door—over Cousin Ebenezer's respectable, conservative and intensely private front-door—hung a large sign-board bearing, in gold letters on a black ground, the inscription:

GALLERY OF CHRISTIAN ART

OPEN ON WEEK-DAYS FROM 2 TO 4
ADMISSION 25 CENTS.   CHILDREN 10 CENTS

Lewis saw his wife turn pale, and pressed her arm in his. "Believe me, it's the only way to make the pictures known. And they *must* be made known," he said with a thrill of his old ardour.

"Yes, dear, of course. But . . . to every one? Publicly?"

"If we showed them only to our friends, of what use would it be? Their opinion is already formed."

She sighed her acknowledgment. "But the . . . the entrance fee . . ."

"If we can afford it later, the gallery will be free. But meanwhile——"

"Oh, Lewis, I quite understand!" And clinging to him, the still-protesting baby in her wake, she passed with a dauntless step under the awful sign-board.

"At last I shall see the pictures properly lighted!" she exclaimed, and turned in the hall to fling her arms about her husband.

"It's all they need . . . to be appreciated," he answered, aglow with her encouragement.

Since his withdrawal from the world it had been a part of Lewis's system never to read the daily papers. His wife eagerly conformed to his example, and they lived in a little air-tight circle of aloofness, as if the cottage at Tarrytown had been situated in another and happier planet.

Lewis, nevertheless, the day after the opening of the Gallery of Christian Art, deemed it his duty to derogate from this attitude, and sallied forth secretly to buy the principal journals. When he re-entered his house he went straight up to the nursery where he knew that, at that hour, Treeshy would be giving the little girl her bath. But it was later than he supposed. The rite was over, the baby lay asleep in its modest cot, and the mother sat crouched by the fire, her face hidden in her hands. Lewis instantly guessed that she too had seen the papers.

"Treeshy—you mustn't . . . consider this of any consequence. . . ," he stammered.

She lifted a tear-stained face. "Oh, my darling! I thought you never read the papers."

"Not usually. But I thought it my duty——"

"Yes; I see. But, as you say, what earthly consequence——?"

"None whatever; we must just be patient and persist."

She hesitated, and then, her arms about him, her head on his breast: "Only, dearest, I've been counting up again, ever so carefully; and even if we give up fires everywhere but in the nursery, I'm afraid the wages of the door-keeper and the guardian . . . especially if the gallery's open to the public every day . . ."

"I've thought of that already, too; and I myself shall hereafter act as doorkeeper and guardian."

He kept his eyes on hers as he spoke. "This is the test," he thought. Her face paled under its brown glow, and the eyes dilated in her effort to check her tears. Then she said gaily: "That will be . . . very interesting, won't it, Lewis? Hearing what the people say. . . . Because, as they begin to know the pictures better, and to understand them, they can't fail to say very interesting things . . . can they?" She turned and caught up the sleeping Louisa. "Can they . . . oh, you darling—darling?"

Lewis turned away too. Not another woman in New York would have been capable of that. He could hear all the town echoing with this new scandal of his showing the pictures himself—and she, so much more sensitive to ridicule, so much less carried away by apostolic ardour, how much louder must that mocking echo ring in her ears! But his pang was only momentary. The one thought that possessed him for any length of time was that of vindicating himself by making the pictures known; he could no longer fix his attention on lesser matters. The derision of illiterate journalists was not a thing to wince at; once let the pictures be seen by educated and intelligent people, and they would speak for themselves—especially if he were at hand to interpret them.

VIII

FOR a week or two a great many people came to the gallery; but, even with Lewis as interpreter, the pictures failed to make themselves heard. During the first days, indeed, owing to the unprecedented idea of holding a paying exhibition in a private house, and to the mockery of the newspapers, the Gallery of Christian Art was thronged with noisy curiosity-seekers; once the astonished metropolitan police had to be invited in to calm their comments and control their movements. But the name of "Christian Art" soon chilled this class of sightseer, and before long they were replaced by a dumb and respectable throng, who roamed vacantly through the rooms and out again, grumbling that it wasn't worth the money. Then these too diminished; and once the tide had turned, the ebb was rapid. Every day from two to four Lewis still sat shivering among his treasures, or patiently measured the length of the deserted gallery: as long as there was a chance of any one coming he would not admit that he was beaten. For the next visitor might always be the one who understood.

One snowy February day he had thus paced the rooms in unbroken solitude for above an hour when carriage-wheels stopped at the door. He hastened to open it, and in a great noise of silks his sister Sarah Anne Huzzard entered.

Lewis felt for a moment as he used to under his father's glance. Marriage and millions had given the moon-faced Sarah something of the Raycie awfulness; but her brother looked into her empty eyes, and his own kept their level.

"Well, Lewis," said Mrs. Huzzard with a simpering sternness, and caught her breath.

"Well, Sarah Anne—I'm happy that you've come to take a look at my pictures."

"I've come to see you and your wife." She gave another nervous gasp, shook out her flounces, and added in a rush: "And to ask you how much longer this . . . this spectacle is to continue. . . ."

"The exhibition?" Lewis smiled. She signed a flushed assent.

"Well, there has been a considerable falling-off lately in the number of visitors——"

"Thank heaven!" she interjected.

"But as long as I feel that any one

wishes to come . . . I shall be here . . .
to open the door, as you see."

She sent a shuddering glance about her.
"Lewis—I wonder if you realize . . . ?"

"Oh, fully."

"Then *why* do you go on? Isn't it
enough—aren't you satisfied?"

"With the effect they have produced?"

"With the effect *you* have produced—
on your family and on the whole of New
York. With the slur on poor Papa's
memory."

"Papa left me the pictures, Sarah
Anne."

"Yes. But not to make yourself a
mountebank about them."

Lewis considered this impartially. "Are
you sure? Perhaps, on the contrary, he
did it for that very reason."

"Oh, don't heap more insults on our
father's memory! Things are bad enough

without that. How your wife can allow
it I can't see. Do you ever consider the
humiliation to *her*?"

Lewis gave another dry smile. "She's
used to being humiliated. The Kents
accustomed her to that."

Sarah Anne reddened. "I don't know
why I should stay to be spoken to in this
way. But I came with my husband's
approval."

"Do you need that to come and see
your brother?"

"I need it to—to make the offer I am
about to make; and which he authorizes."

Lewis looked at her in surprise, and she
purpled up to the lace ruffles inside her
satin bonnet.

"Have you come to make an offer for
my collection?" he asked her, humorously.

"You seem to take pleasure in insinuat-
ing preposterous things. But anything

is better than this public slight on our name." Again she ran a shuddering glance over the pictures. "John and I," she announced, "are prepared to double the allowance mother left you on condition that this . . . this ends . . . for good. That that horrible sign is taken down tonight."

Lewis seemed mildly to weigh the proposal. "Thank you very much, Sarah Anne," he said at length. "I'm touched . . . touched and . . . and surprised . . . that you and John should have made this offer. But perhaps, before I decline it, you will accept *mine*: simply to show you my pictures. When once you've looked at them I think you'll understand——"

Mrs. Huzzard drew back hastily, her air of majesty collapsing. "Look at the pictures? Oh, thank you . . . but I can

see them very well from here. And besides, I don't pretend to be a judge . . ."

"Then come up and see Treeshy and
the baby," said Lewis quietly.

She stared at him, embarrassed. "Oh,
thank you," she stammered again; and
as she prepared to follow him: "Then it's
no, really no, Lewis? Do consider, my
dear! You say yourself that hardly any
one comes. What harm can there be in
closing the place?"

"What—when tomorrow the man may
come who understands?"

Mrs. Huzzard tossed her plumes de-
spairingly and followed him in silence.

"What—Mary Adeline?" she exclaimed,
pausing abruptly on the threshold of the
nursery. Treeshy, as usual, sat holding
her baby by the fire; and from a low seat
opposite her rose a lady as richly furred
and feathered as Mrs. Huzzard, but with

far less assurance to carry off her furbelows. Mrs. Kent ran to Lewis and laid her plump cheek against his, while Treeshy greeted Sarah Anne.

"I had no idea you were here, Mary Adeline," Mrs. Huzzard murmured. It was clear that she had not imparted her philanthropic project to her sister, and was disturbed at the idea that Lewis might be about to do so. "I just dropped in for a minute," she continued, "to see that darling little pet of an angel child—" and she enveloped the astonished baby in her ample rustlings and flutterings.

"I'm very glad to see you here, Sarah Anne," Mary Adeline answered with simplicity.

"Ah, it's not for want of wishing that I haven't come before! Treeshy knows that, I hope. But the cares of a household like mine . . ."

"Yes; and it's been so difficult to get about in the bad weather," Treeshy suggested sympathetically.

Mrs. Huzzard lifted the Raycie eyebrows. "Has it really? With two pairs of horses one hardly notices the weather. . . Oh, the pretty, pretty, *pretty* baby! . . . Mary Adeline," Sarah Anne continued, turning severely to her sister, "I shall be happy to offer you a seat in my carriage if you're thinking of leaving."

But Mary Adeline was a married woman too. She raised her mild head and her glance crossed her sister's quietly. "My own carriage is at the door, thank you kindly, Sarah Anne," she said; and the baffled Sarah Anne withdrew on Lewis's arm. But a moment later the old habit of subordination reasserted itself. Mary Adeline's gentle countenance grew as

timorous as a child's, and she gathered up
her cloak in haste.

"Perhaps I was too quick. . . I'm
sure she meant it kindly," she exclaimed,
overtaking Lewis as he turned to come up
the stairs; and with a smile he stood watching his two sisters drive off together in the
Huzzard coach.

He returned to the nursery, where
Treeshy was still crooning over her
daughter.

"Well, my dear," he said, "what do you
suppose Sarah Anne came for?" And, in
reply to her wondering gaze: "To buy me
off from showing the pictures!"

His wife's indignation took just the
form he could have wished. She simply
went on with her rich cooing laugh and
hugged the baby tighter. But Lewis felt
the perverse desire to lay a still greater
strain upon her loyalty.

"Offered to double my allowance, she and John, if only I'll take down the sign!"

"No one shall touch the sign!" Treeshy flamed.

"Not till I do," said her husband grimly.

She turned about and scanned him with anxious eyes. "Lewis . . . *you?*"

"Oh, my dear . . . they're right. . . It can't go on forever . . ." He went up to her, and put his arm about her and the child. "You've been braver than an army of heroes; but it won't do. The expenses have been a good deal heavier than I was led to expect. And I . . . I can't raise a mortgage on the pictures. Nobody will touch them."

She met this quickly. "No; I know. That was what Mary Adeline came about."

The blood rushed angrily to Lewis's temples. "Mary Adeline—how the devil did *she* hear of it?"

"Through Mr. Reedy, I suppose. But you must not be angry. She was kindness itself: she doesn't want you to close the gallery, Lewis . . . that is, not as long as you really continue to believe in it. . . She and Donald Kent will lend us enough to go on with for a year longer. That is what she came to say."

For the first time since the struggle had begun, Lewis Raycie's throat was choked with tears. His faithful Mary Adeline! He had a sudden vision of her, stealing out of the house at High Point before daylight to carry a basket of scraps to the poor Mrs. Edgar Poe who was dying of a decline down the lane. . . He laughed aloud in his joy.

"Dear old Mary Adeline! How magnificent of her! Enough to give me a whole year more . . ." He pressed his wet cheek against his wife's in a long silence. "Well, dear," he said at length, "it's for you to say—do we accept?"

He held her off, questioningly, at arm's length, and her wan little smile met his own and mingled with it.

"Of course we accept!"

O F the Raycie family, which pre-
vailed so powerfully in the New
York of the 'forties, only one of the name
survived in my boyhood, half a century
later. Like so many of the descendants
of the proud little Colonial society, the
Raycies had totally vanished, forgotten by
everyone but a few old ladies, one or two
genealogists and the sexton of Trinity
Church, who kept the record of their
graves.

The Raycie blood was of course still to
be traced in various allied families: Kents,
Huzzards, Cosbys and many others, proud
to claim cousinship with a "Signer," but
already indifferent or incurious as to the
fate of his progeny. These old New

Yorkers, who lived so well and spent their money so liberally, vanished like a pinch of dust when they disappeared from their pews and their dinner-tables.

If I happen to have been familiar with the name since my youth, it is chiefly because its one survivor was a distant cousin of my mother's, whom she sometimes took me to see on days when she thought I was likely to be good because I had been promised a treat for the morrow.

Old Miss Alethea Raycie lived in a house I had always heard spoken of as "Cousin Ebenezer's." It had evidently, in its day, been an admired specimen of domestic architecture; but was now regarded as the hideous though venerable relic of a bygone age. Miss Raycie, being crippled by rheumatism, sat above stairs in a large cold room, meagrely furnished with beadwork tables, rosewood étagères and portraits of pale sad-looking people in odd clothes. She herself was large and saturnine, with a battlemented black lace cap, and so deaf that she seemed a survival of forgotten days, a Rosetta Stone to which the clue was lost. Even to my mother, nursed in that vanished tradition, and knowing instinctively to whom Miss Raycie alluded when she spoke of Mary Adeline, Sarah Anne or Uncle Doctor, intercourse with her was difficult and languishing, and my juvenile interruptions were oftener encouraged than reproved.

In the course of one of these visits my eye, listlessly roaming, singled out among the pallid portraits a three-crayon drawing of a little girl with a large forehead and dark eyes, dressed in a plaid frock and embroidered pantalettes, and sitting on a grass-bank. I pulled my mother's sleeve to ask who she was, and my mother answered: "Ah, that was poor little Louisa Raycie, who died of a decline. How old was little Louisa when she died, Cousin Alethea?"

To batter this simple question into Cousin Alethea's brain was the affair of ten laborious minutes; and when the job was done, and Miss Raycie, with an air of mysterious displeasure, had dropped a deep "Eleven," my mother was too exhausted to continue. So she turned to me to add, with one of the private smiles we kept for each other: "It was the poor child who would have inherited the Raycie Gallery." But to a little boy of my age this item of information lacked interest, nor did I understand my mother's surreptitious amusement.

This far-off scene suddenly came back to me last year, when, on one of my infrequent visits to New York, I went to dine with my old friend, the banker, John Selwyn, and came to an astonished stand before the mantelpiece in his new library.

"Hal*lo*!" I said, looking up at the picture above the chimney.

My host squared his shoulders, thrust his hands into his pockets, and affected the air of modesty which people think it proper to assume when their possessions are admired. "The Macrino d'Alba? Y—yes . . . it was the only thing I managed to capture out of the Raycie collection."

"The only thing? Well——"

"Ah, but you should have seen the Mantegna; *and* the Giotto; *and* the Piero della Francesca—hang it, one of the most beautiful Piero della Francescas in the world. . . A girl in profile, with her hair in a pearl net, against a background of columbines; *that* went back to Europe—

the National Gallery, I believe. And the Carpaccio, the most exquisite little St. George . . . that went to California . . . *Lord!*" He sat down with the sigh of a hungry man turned away from a groaning board. "Well, it nearly broke me buying *this!*" he murmured, as if at least that fact were some consolation.

I was turning over my early memories in quest of a clue to what he spoke of as the Raycie collection, in a tone which implied that he was alluding to objects familiar to all art-lovers.

Suddenly: "They weren't poor little Louisa's pictures, by any chance?" I asked, remembering my mother's cryptic smile.

Sedwyn looked at me perplexedly. "Who the deuce is poor little Louisa?" And, without waiting for my answer, he went on: "They were that fool Netta

Cosby's until a year ago—and she never
even knew it."

We looked at each other interrogatively,
my friend perplexed at my ignorance, and
I now absorbed in trying to run down the
genealogy of Netta Cosby. I did so finally.
"Netta Cosby—you don't mean Netta
Kent, the one who married Jim Cosby?"

"That's it. They were cousins of the
Raycies', and she inherited the pictures."

I continued to ponder. "I wanted
awfully to marry her, the year I left Har-
vard," I said presently, more to myself
than to my hearer.

"Well, if you had you'd have annexed
a prize fool; *and* one of the most beautiful
collections of Italian Primitives in the
world."

"In the world?"

"Well—you wait till you see them; if
you haven't already. And I seem to make

out that you haven't—that you can't have.
How long have you been in Japan? Four
years? I thought so. Well, it was only
last winter that Netta found out."

"Found out what?"

"What there was in old Alethea Raycie's attic. You must remember the old
Miss Raycie who lived in that hideous
house in Tenth Street when we were children. She was a cousin of your mother's,
wasn't she? Well, the old fool lived there
for nearly half a century, with five millions' worth of pictures shut up in the
attic over her head. It seems they'd been
there ever since the death of a poor young
Raycie who collected them in Italy years
and years ago. I don't know much about
the story; I never was strong on genealogy, and the Raycies have always been
rather dim to me. They were everybody's
cousins, of course; but as far as one can

make out that seems to have been their principal if not their only function. Oh— and I suppose the Raycie Building was called after them; only *they* didn't build it!

"But there was this one young fellow— I wish I could find out more about him. All that Netta seems to know (or to care, for that matter) is that when he was very young—barely out of college—he was sent to Italy by his father to buy Old Masters —in the 'forties, it must have been— and came back with this extraordinary, this unbelievable collection . . . a boy of that age! . . . and was disinherited by the old gentleman for bringing home such rubbish. The young fellow and his wife died ever so many years ago, both of them. It seems he was so laughed at for buying such pictures that they went away and lived like hermits in the depths of the country. There were some funny spectral

portraits of them that old Alethea had up
in her bedroom. Netta showed me one of
them the last time I went to see her: a
pathetic drawing of the only child, an
anæmic little girl with a big forehead.
Jove, but that must have been your little
Louisa!"

I nodded. "In a plaid frock and embroidered pantalettes?"

"Yes, something of the sort. Well,
when Louisa and her parents died, I suppose the pictures went to old Miss Raycie.
At any rate, at some time or other—and it
must have been longer ago than you or
I can remember—the old lady inherited
them with the Tenth Street house; and
when *she* died, three or four years ago, her
relations found she'd never even been up-
stairs to look at them."

"Well——?"

"Well, she died intestate, and Netta

Kent—Netta Cosby—turned out to be
the next of kin. There wasn't much to be
got out of the estate (or so they thought)
and, as the Cosbys are always hard up,
the house in Tenth Street had to be sold,
and the pictures were very nearly sent off
to the auction room with all the rest of the
stuff. But nobody supposed they would
bring anything, and the auctioneer said
that if you tried to sell pictures with carpets and bedding and kitchen furniture it
always depreciated the whole thing; and
so, as the Cosbys had some bare walls to
cover, they sent for the lot—there were
about thirty—and decided to have them
cleaned and hang them up. 'After all,'
Netta said, 'as well as I can make out
through the cobwebs, some of them look
like rather jolly copies of early Italian
things.' But as she was short of cash she
decided to clean them at home instead of

sending them to an expert; and one day, while she was operating on this very one before you, with her sleeves rolled up, the man called who always *does* call on such occasions; the man who knows. In the given case, it was a quiet fellow connected with the Louvre, who'd brought her a letter from Paris, and whom she'd invited to one of her stupid dinners. He was announced, and she thought it would be a joke to let him see what she was doing; she has pretty arms, you may remember. So he was asked into the dining-room, where he found her with a pail of hot water and soap-suds, and *this* laid out on the table; and the first thing he did was to grab her pretty arm so tight that it was black and blue, while he shouted out: 'God in heaven! Not *hot* water!' "

My friend leaned back with a sigh of mingled resentment and satisfaction, and we sat silently looking up at the lovely "Adoration" above the mantelpiece.

"That's how I got it a little cheaper— most of the old varnish was gone for good. But luckily for her it was the first picture she had attacked; and as for the others—you must see them, that's all I can say. . . Wait; I've got the catalogue somewhere about . . ."

He began to rummage for it, and I asked, remembering how nearly I had married Netta Kent: "Do you mean to say she didn't keep a single one of them?"

"Oh, yes—in the shape of pearls and Rolls-Royces. And you've seen their new house in Fifth Avenue?" He ended with a grin of irony: "The best of the joke is that Jim was just thinking of divorcing her when the pictures were discovered."

"Poor little Louisa!" I sighed.

(5)

THE END